THE BEAR SANTA CLAUS FORGOT

by Diana Kimpton
Illustrated by Anna Kiernan

Cartwheel
·B·O·O·K·S·®

SCHOLASTIC INC.
New York   Toronto   London   Auckland   Sydney

To Madeleine – DK
For my Mum and Dad with love – AK

First published in 1994 by Scholastic Publications Ltd.
Text copyright © 1994 by Diana Kimpton.
Illustrations copyright © 1994 by Anna Kiernan.
All rights reserved. Published by Scholastic Inc., 555 Broadway, New York, NY 10012
by arrangement with Scholastic Publications Ltd.
CARTWHEEL BOOKS and the CARTWHEEL BOOKS logo
are registered trademarks of Scholastic Inc.

Library of Congress Cataloging-in-Publication Data

Kimpton, Diana.
  [Bear Father Christmas forgot]
  The bear Santa Claus forgot / by Diana Kimpton; illustrated by Anna Kiernan.
     p.   cm.
  "Cartwheel Books."
  Summary: A teddy bear that Santa is supposed to deliver to a little girl falls out of
his bag of toys, and the bear must find his own way to the girl in time for Christmas
morning.
  ISBN 0-590-26564-4
  [1. Christmas—Fiction.   2. Teddy bears—Fiction.   3. Santa Claus—Fiction.]
I. Kiernan, Anna, ill.   II. Title.
PZ7.K56494Be   1994
[E]—dc20   94-37247
                                                                       CIP
                                                                        AC

12 11 10 9 8 7 6 5 4 3 2 1   5 6 7 8 9/9 0/0

Printed in Belgium

First Scholastic printing, October 1995

Christmas Eve was almost over. Santa Claus yawned. Just one more visit to make and then he could go home. The sleigh landed gently on Maddie's roof. Santa Claus put the last few toys into a sack and swung it onto his back. But the sack was old. It had a hole in one corner.

"OH NO!" said the bear, as he slid through the hole.

"OUCH," said the bear, as he landed with a bump on the floor of the sleigh.

He sat up and rubbed his head.

He could see Santa Claus climbing down Maddie's chimney without him.

That wasn't right. He was Maddie's bear. The tag around his neck said so. She had asked Santa Claus for him weeks ago. What would she say in the morning when he wasn't there?

For
Maddie

When Santa came back, he didn't notice the teddy bear sitting all by himself. He just climbed onto the sleigh and whistled to his reindeer. They galloped away, pulling the sleigh into the night sky.

First the sleigh turned to the right.

"Oops," said the bear, as he tumbled across the floor.

"Ouch," said the bear, as he bumped into the side of the sleigh.

Then the sleigh turned to the left.

"Oops," said the bear, as he tumbled across the floor.

"Ouch," said the bear, as he bumped into the other side of the sleigh.

Then the front of the sleigh pointed up into the air, as the reindeer galloped higher and higher.

"Oops," said the bear, as he tumbled across the floor.

"Help!" cried the bear, as he bounced out of the back of the sleigh.

The bear grabbed desperately for something to
save him. As the sleigh flew off, the teddy bear
dangled from the back by his front paws.

"Whew!" said the bear, as he held on very tight. His paws hurt, but at least he was safe. Then he looked down and saw the roof of Maddie's house far below him. *That's where I should be*, he thought. *If Santa won't take me, I'll have to go by myself.*

The bear shut his eyes and let go.

"Aaargh!" cried the bear, as he fell through the air. "Oh!" said the bear, as he whirled around and around, his arms and legs flying in all directions.

"Ouch," said the bear, as he landed with a thump on Maddie's roof.

He sat up and brushed some snow off the end of his nose. The snow was cold and wet. It made his fur all spiky.

The bear climbed up onto a pile of snow and looked down the chimney.

Inside it was dark and scary. He didn't want to go down there, but how else could he get into Maddie's house?

"Oooh," said the bear, as he climbed into the chimney's dark opening.

"Aargh!" cried the bear, as he slid down the chimney.

"Ouch," said the bear, as he landed in the fireplace in a cloud of soot and ash.

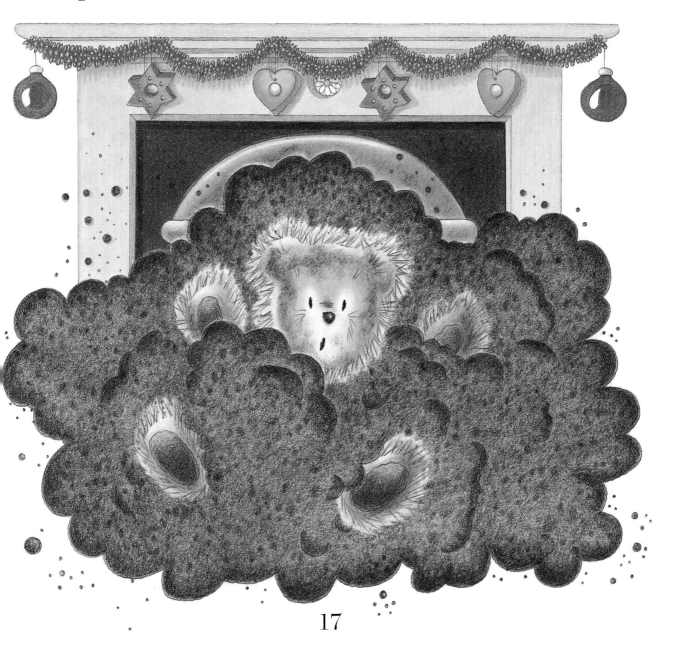

There was no Christmas stocking by the fireplace. *It must be in Maddie's room,* thought the bear, so he started to climb the stairs....

The stairs were very tall for a bear. The stairs were very steep for a bear.

"Whew," said the bear, when he got to the top. He wanted to stop for a rest, but he couldn't. He had to hurry. It was almost Christmas morning.

He walked softly down the hallway and peeked around the first door.

"Hmmm," said the bear, with a shake of his head. He could hear water dripping. He could smell soap.

This wasn't Maddie's room.

He peeked around the second door. "Hmmm," said the bear, with a shake of his head. He could see a big bed with two people in it. He could hear someone snoring.

This wasn't Maddie's room.

He peeked around the third door. "Ah-ha," said the bear. He could see a little girl fast asleep. He could see a Christmas stocking hanging on the end of her bed.

This must be Maddie's room.

But the stocking was very high for a bear.

"Oh," said the bear, with a tear in his eye. There was no way he could get into Maddie's stocking. There was no way he could be a true Christmas present, unless…

"Hmmm," said the bear, as he scratched his head thoughtfully. In the corner of the room were some leftover decorations.

"Oh boy!" said the bear, as he rolled himself up in a sheet of wrapping paper.

"Oops!" said the bear, as he fell flat on his back.

"At last," said the bear, as he looked up at the stocking. He was badly wrapped, a little damp and a bit dirty, but he was in just the right place—well, almost, anyway.

That's where Maddie found him in the morning…

and she loved him right away.